The Boy who was Raised by Librarians

Written by Carla Morris • Illustrated by Brad Sneed

LIVINGSTON LIBRARY

Published by
PEACHTREE PUBLISHERS
1700 Chattahoochee Avenue
Atlanta, Georgia 30318-2112
www.peachtree-online.com

Text © 2007 by Carla Morris
Illustrations © 2007 by Brad Sneed

Book and cover design by Brad Sneed
Art direction by Loraine M. Joyner
Typesetting by Melanie McMahon Ives

The illustrations were created in watercolor and gouache
on 140# hot press watercolor paper

Printed in Singapore
10 9 8 7

Library of Congress Cataloging-in-Publication Data

Morris, Carla D.
  The boy who was raised by librarians / written by Carla Morris ; illustrated by
Brad Sneed. -- 1st ed.
      p. cm.
  Summary: Melvin discovers that the public library is the place where he can
find just about anything--including three librarians who help in his quest for
knowledge.
  ISBN 13: 978-1-56145-391-7
  ISBN 10: 1-56145-391-9
[1. Librarians--Fiction. 2. Libraries--Fiction.] I. Sneed, Brad, ill. II. Title.
  PZ7.M8272435Bo 2007
  [E]--dc22
                              2006024279

To children's librarians everywhere—
may you be comforted by the knowledge that your
daily small acts of kindness and service to children
will result in adults who will do the same!
And also to Ian Perkes, who grew up
in the Provo City Library.
—C. M.

To Mom and Dad
—B. S.

PEACHTREE
ATLANTA

Melvin lived in the Livingston Public Library.
Well…he didn't really live there. He just spent lots and lots of time there.

He wanted to know a little…no…a lot about everything. He was curious. And the library is a wonderful place to be if a person is curious.

Everything had its place in the library and Melvin liked it that way. His favorite books were always in their places, lined up on the shelves like soldiers. And his favorite people were always in their places, behind the reference desk.

W hen Melvin was barely tall enough to see over the counter, he started going to the library after school every day.

He made sure to stop by the reference desk for a chat with the librarians.
They were always happy to see him.

"Hi Melvin!" Marge said.

"How was school today?" Betty asked.

"How's the weather out there?" asked Leeola.

Melvin loved the librarians. Whatever he was interested in, they were interested in it too.

"Where can I find some information about snakes?" he asked one afternoon.

"Well," said Marge. "How would you like to raise a snake all by yourself? Here's a great book: *Raising Snakes in Your Bathtub: From Cute, Baby Racers to Big, Ugly Cobras.*"

Betty chimed in, "Here, dear, an arts and crafts book: *Making Snakeskin Purses, Shoes, and Other Matching Accessories.*"

"Hey! *Snake Poems and Blessings,*" added Leeola, as she found forty-two snake websites with just three keystrokes.

That's how librarians are. They just can't help it. And that's why Melvin loved them.

In first grade, Melvin and his class went on a field trip…to a real field.

That afternoon, he ran to the library to show his friends his treasure—a big Mason jar filled with all kinds of bugs.

"Look what I have!" he called, as he burst through the library doors. "Can you help me identify them?"

MELLLLLVIN!

Melvin TRIPPED,

All eighty-seven specimens of caterpillars, cooties, and creepy crawlies were loose in the Livingston Public Library!

Marge, Betty, and Leeola quickly organized an emergency rescue squad. The bugs were retrieved, identified, classified, and cataloged within twenty minutes.

"How'd you do that so fast?" asked Melvin.

"That's how we are," explained Leeola.

"When we see chaos…," began Betty.

"…we organize and catalog," finished Marge. "It's in our nature." She pulled out *A Field Guide to Insects* and handed it to Melvin.

To apologize, Melvin gave the librarians a lovely bouquet of flowers—picked from the library's garden.

Then he stopped to examine the aquarium next to the circulation desk.

"Don't put your hand in the fish tank," Marge warned him.

"But I was wondering," said Melvin, "How many kinds of fish are in the whole world and all the lakes and all the rivers and all the seas? And how much does the whole world with all the dogs and cats and houses and cars and tractors weigh?"

The librarians were very busy with other patrons, but Leeola knew just where to find some answers for Melvin. She sat down at the computer with Melvin and they found the answers together.

She couldn't help it. That's how librarians are.

In second grade, Melvin was cast as the Enormous Eggplant in the school play. He practiced his part with the librarians.

"Now say your line again," said Leeola, as she shelved the new Caldecott Award winners.

"Project your voice to the back of the auditorium," said Marge, in an alarmingly loud and clear voice.

"But be natural!" said Betty. "Try to look like you're not acting." She read aloud from *Organic Gardening* magazine to help him find his motivation.

The audience gave the Enormous Eggplant a standing ovation.

Melvin attended all the library programs. He was always the first person to complete the Summer Reading Program. He loved the After School Specials and the Readerguys Book Club and Movie Nights. He came to all the story hours, no matter the hour.

But the Spend the Night in the Library party was the best! Betty read the kids a bedtime story.

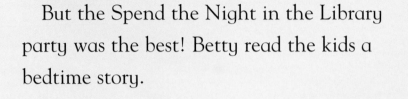

Melvin curled up in his sleeping bag near the encyclopedias. Surrounded by thousands of books, he felt rich and happy.

In third grade, Melvin started a baseball card collection. He would spread the cards out on a table in the library and organize them into teams, players, and rookies.

Betty showed him how to store them in acid-free, archival-approved boxes, and Leeola found him a price guide on the internet.

They couldn't help it. That's how librarians are.

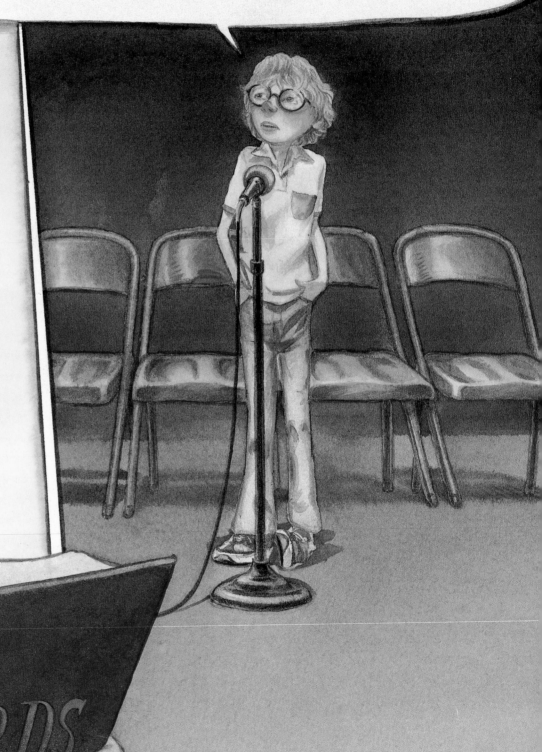

In fourth grade, Melvin entered The Complete and Unabridged A-to-Z Spelling Bee. Marge suggested he read the 100th edition of *Words to Know* every day after school.

Not surprisingly, he won first place.

In fifth grade, Melvin won both the gold and silver trophies in the Know Every Town, City, State, and Country in the Solar System Geography Contest.

Marge, Betty, and Leeola were so proud of him. They couldn't help it. That's how librarians are.

In sixth grade, Melvin entered the
Extraordinary, Completely-Out-of-
Your-Mind Science Fair. The librarians
helped him find information about all
the projects that had ever won. Melvin
came up with a winner.

In seventh grade, he was picked to be on "So You Want to Be the Smartest Kid." Marge, Betty, and Leeola burst with pride as Melvin answered questions so fast that he blew out the circuits on the computer keeping score.

Every day after school, year after year, Melvin came to the library. When he was in high school, he even got a part-time job there.

Marge, Betty, and Leeola cried with pride and happiness at Melvin's graduation.
"That's our boy," said Marge.
"We helped him learn," said Betty.
"All those books," said Leeola.

After Melvin left for college, he missed the Livingston Library and his librarian friends. He wrote them letters and e-mails about the books he was reading and the things he was learning.

Years later, another boy came to the Livingston Public Library…and loved it.

"Hi, Sterling," Marge said.

"How was the field trip?" Betty asked.

"Do you need help identifying those bugs?" asked Leeola.

"We can identify, organize, and catalog in no time.
We can't help it," said Livingston's newest librarian.
"That's how we are!"